DO YOU KNOW WHAT MAGIC IS?

Stories and Songs by
LINDA ARNOLD

Illustrations by
JENNY JO MOORE

PRICE STERN SLOAN
Los Angeles

To my magical children,
Katy and Toby
—L.A.

To my nieces and nephews
—J.J.M.

Text and illustrations copyright © 1988 by Linda Arnold
Song lyrics copyright © 1988 by Arnold Music Publishing
Published by Price Stern Sloan, Inc.
360 North La Cienega Boulevard, Los Angeles, California   90048

ISBN 0-8431-1946-2

DO YOU KNOW WHAT MAGIC IS?

There were some kids and a short giraffe
Skipping along a crooked path
Close behind, a happy clown
Was gently tip-toeing around
Well, they came to a candy store
Bought some gumdrops and balloons
And turned into moons

    Chorus:

        Oh, do you know what magic is?
        Have you been to rainbow land?
        Or seen a dinosaur go sailing by?
        Any kid can help you try

There were some kids on a
      merry-go-round
They rode their ponies all over town
They had some birthday cake and pizza pie
Poor little Michael got an olive in his eye
Then they rode off in the wind
And called their wooden ponies
"Pepperonies"

    Chorus

There were some kids at a movie show
They took their seats and it started to snow
And then it rained all over the place
Poor little Jenny got ice cream on her face
Then they opened their umbrellas
And they flew off in the sun
Just having fun

    Chorus

JENNY AND THE MAGIC HORSE

O ne beautiful summer day Jennifer Elizabeth Peabody went out to explore the woods and meadows behind her new home. She was hoping to find some dinosaur bones, or maybe a slippery salamander, when she noticed an old wishing well.

"Hello, down there!" she shouted into the darkness of the well.

Jennifer wondered how far it was to the bottom. She picked up a stone and was about to drop it in, when a strange little voice gurgled, "Hello, up there!"

Jennifer couldn't believe her ears! She looked around in every direction to see who could have spoken. Except for some playful squirrels, there was no one in sight.

"Well, go ahead, make your wish," the silly voice continued. It was definitely coming from the well! "I haven't got all day, you know."

Jenny had always had the unfortunate habit of sneezing great big sneezes whenever she was startled or confused, and this was no exception. "Ah..ah..ahchoo!"

KERPLOP, went the stone from Jenny's hand.

"Ouch!" cried the voice in the well.

"Oh, excuse me," Jenny quickly apologized. "I didn't mean to . . ."

"Never mind," the odd voice interrupted. "It's part of my job. You'd be amazed at what people throw down here. Just look at all this junk!"

Jenny jumped quickly out of the way as a tower of water came shooting up from the bottom of the well. Floating about in the surprising fountain were all sorts of ridiculous things: baseballs, boomerangs, fishing poles, frying pans and more . . .

"See what I mean!" the well complained. "You don't have to get fancy to make a wish, one penny will do. In fact, one tear means more to me than all the treasures in the world."

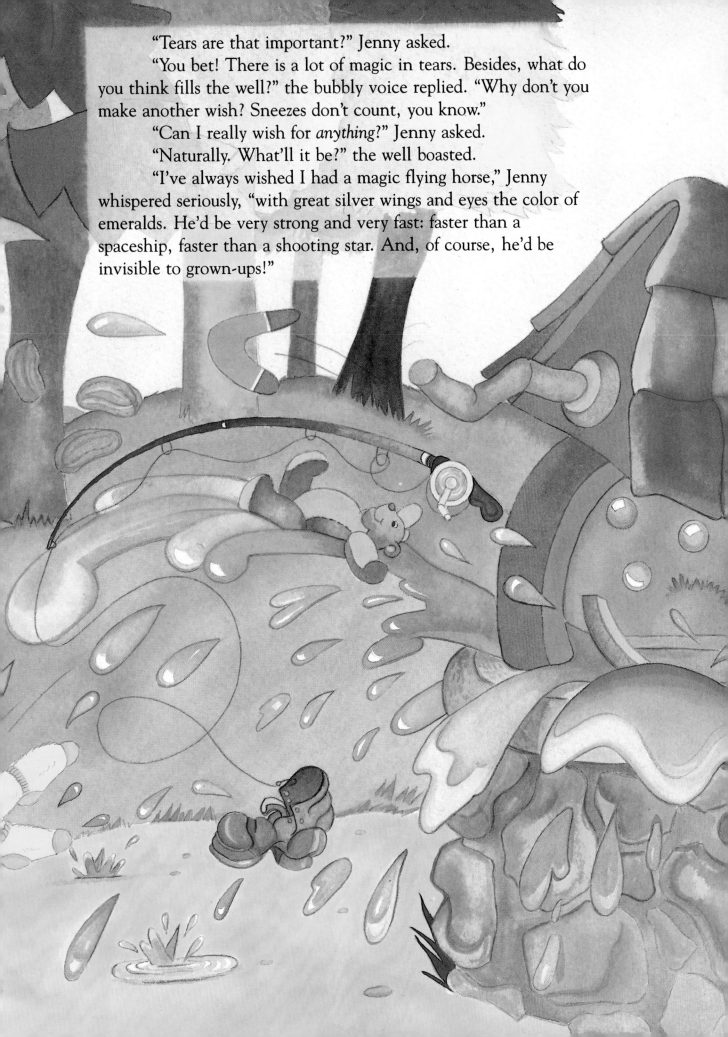

"Tears are that important?" Jenny asked.

"You bet! There is a lot of magic in tears. Besides, what do you think fills the well?" the bubbly voice replied. "Why don't you make another wish? Sneezes don't count, you know."

"Can I really wish for *anything*?" Jenny asked.

"Naturally. What'll it be?" the well boasted.

"I've always wished I had a magic flying horse," Jenny whispered seriously, "with great silver wings and eyes the color of emeralds. He'd be very strong and very fast: faster than a spaceship, faster than a shooting star. And, of course, he'd be invisible to grown-ups!"

"Of course!" laughed the well. "I think I've got the picture. One magic horse coming right up."

Jenny heard some rumble-grumble noises from inside the well. A cloud of smoke appeared and, POOF, there stood a monkey dressed in pink sneakers and purple sunglasses!

"Oh, drat!" yelled the well. "Let me try again."

There was another cloud of smoke and this time, instead of a monkey, POOF, a gigantic snail appeared. It was three feet tall and it oozed bubbly slime as it slithered in Jenny's direction.

"Yuck!" cried Jenny.

"Bother!" snapped the well.

"If it's too much trouble . . ." Jenny began, cautiously moving to the other side of the well.

"Of course!" shouted the well, "I forgot to use the magic words."

There was more rumble-grumble this time, followed by, "Zippity, Bippity, Bubbly-Boo, Snippity-Snap, Wish Come True!" Suddenly a bolt of lightning and a blast of thunder shook the ground. Jenny watched, spellbound, as a magnificent silver horse streaked down from the clouds.

"Oh, thank you, Mr. Well. Thank you." Jenny exclaimed.

"No trouble," he replied. "By the way, the name's Willard, but you can call me Willie."

The horse rubbed his nose gently on Jenny's shoulder and whinnied softly. "I think he likes me," she laughed.

"Don't just stand there," Willie the well answered. "Go for a ride!"

Jenny climbed onto his smooth back and, WHEE, off they went. Faster than a spaceship, faster than a shooting star, flew Jennifer Peabody on her magic horse. As they soared above the earth Jenny noticed a beautiful rainbow reaching toward an island in the clouds.

"Is that where you come from?" Jenny asked her flying friend.

The horse gave a playful whinny, and before she had time for more questions they landed softly on a beach of amazing rainbow-colored sand. Splashing about in the waves were other wonderful horses. They all turned their heads as Jenny and her horse galloped along the edge of the water.

"Hold on tight, Jennifer," the magic horse whinnied.

Suddenly all the other horses charged up beside them and the race was on.

"Yipee!" shouted Jenny as they finished ahead of the others. "You're the greatest magic horse ever!"

Soon it was time to take flight again, but not before Jenny had filled her pockets with rainbow sand.

As they sailed through a fluffy cloud, Jenny laughed, "My brother, Michael, will never believe this."

They were flying over the part of the forest where Jenny had met the well when she saw smoke billowing up from the trees.

"The lightning must have set the forest on fire! We've got to do something!" she shouted. Hovering over her head Jenny saw a dark rain cloud.

"Let's go!" she shouted, and off they soared, right into the middle of that thick, black cloud. Back and forth they flew as Jenny scattered handfuls of rainbow sand into the wet cloud. Her pockets were nearly empty when, WHOOSH, the cloud burst open and rain poured down on the burning forest.

In no time the fire was completely out. When Jenny and her horse landed they saw thick grey clouds of steam and ash pouring out of the well.

Jenny jumped from her horse and ran to the well. "Willie! Please speak to me! Are you there, Willie?" But this time there was no answer.

As one big tear rolled down Jennifer's cheek and fell into the smoky well, she sobbed, "Oh, Willie, I wish you were still here. I wish this fire had never happened."

POOF!

The soot was gone, the smoke cleared, the forest was green again and the squirrels were playing in the trees. Jenny threw her arms around the magic horse shouting, "There really is a lot of magic in tears!"

"You bet there is!" answered a familiar bubbly voice. "It's a well kept secret everyone should know." Because Jenny had saved the well's life, she was granted another wish. This time she wished that she and Willie would always be friends. And so they are, to this very day.

THERE'S A LOT OF MAGIC IN TEARS

There's a lot of magic in tears
So don't be afraid to cry
If you have a wish let your tears
Give it wings to fly

There's a lot of magic in tears
Your heart will tell you so
If you feel you need to cry
Just let go

Tears can calm you when you're feeling mad
Tears can help you wash away the sad
And sometimes tears come bubbling up
When you're feeling glad

There's a lot of magic in tears
So don't be afraid to cry
If you have a wish let your tears
Give it wings to fly

There's no need for you to try and hide
The tears that come from down deep inside
For every real tear has a way
Of brightening up your day

There's a lot of magic in tears
Your heart will tell you so
If you feel you need to cry
Just let go

If you have a special wish
You want to make come true
Just be sure that when you wish
Your heart is wishing too

There's a lot of magic in tears
Oooh, Oooh, Oooh

Now, every once in a while, when Jennifer Elizabeth Peabody goes to her bedroom window to look out at the night stars, she sees the magnificent horse with great silver wings and eyes the color of emeralds flying toward her, faster than a spaceship, faster than a shooting star, across the face of the moon.

MAGIC HORSE

If I had a magic horse
Just think what I could do
Climb upon its silver back
And sail the skies of blue

Above the mountains high
My horse and I would fly
To a land far away
Where magic horses run and play

   Chorus:

   Oh, if I had a magic horse
   He'd be my best friend
   Together we would sail away
   To the rainbow's end
   Oh, to the rainbow's end

On sunny days we would play
Beside the deep blue sea
He would be invisible
To everyone but me

Along the silver sand
He'd nibble from my hand
Laughing out loud
We'd dance and prance right
through a cloud

   Chorus

Some nights I would wait for him
By the window of my room
Watching for his silhouette
Across the silver moon

Swiftly he'd fly
Gently to my side
Like a shooting star
Into the night we'd travel far

   Chorus

MICHAEL AND THE MARVELOUS TIME FACTORY

"I wonder if anyone cares that tomorrow is my birthday?" Michael James Peabody whispered as he sat gazing at the stars from his bedroom window. With the silent night sky above him, Michael began to feel more and more lonely.

"What good is a birthday party without any friends?" he sighed. Michael's family had recently moved to the country from their city apartment, so the only friend invited to his party was his older sister, Jenny . . . and sisters don't really count.

"Oh, who cares about having a birthday party and fun anyway!" Michael said as he lay his head on the pillow and closed his eyes. He didn't see the brilliant shooting star that blazed across the sky at that very moment.

HONK, HONK!

Michael had just finished dressing the next morning when he saw a rickety old truck pull up to his front door. On the side of the truck he read the letters, UPS. Beneath that there were smaller letters that spelled, UNBELIEVABLE PARCEL SERVICE. The door of the truck swung open and out popped an odd little man dressed in brightly colored overalls and a cap.

"Is this 123 Pickleberry Lane, home of Michael James Peabody?" he asked when Michael opened the door.

"Yes. I'm Michael Peabody," Michael replied.

"Wonderful!" said the cheerful driver, "I have your order."

Before Michael could ask "What order?" the little man was pulling a large box, wrapped with a shiny blue ribbon, out of the truck. Michael heard knocking from inside the box.

"Quiet down, Grandpa," the driver chuckled, as he wheeled the mysterious package into the front hall.

Grandpa? Michael thought, and he felt his stomach begin to tighten. Could there really be an old man in there?

"Up to his old tricks again," laughed the driver. As he lifted the lid of the noisy box Michael saw a beautiful old grandfather clock!

"He'll keep good time . . . when he wants to, that is!" the driver said, with a wink. Then, reaching into his pocket, he handed Michael a shiny brass key. "You'll be needing this," said the little man and tipping his cap, he and his rickety truck disappeared down Pickleberry Lane.

Michael held the small key up to the light and read the words on it. KEEPER OF THE TIME. He wasn't sure what that meant, but he thought the key might open the door in the front of the clock. As he was about to try it, his mother came into the hall.

"What on earth is this doing here?" she exclaimed.

"UPS," Michael answered, trying to sound matter-of-fact. While his mother went to call the parcel

service, Michael quietly slipped the key into the lock. As he began to turn it, waves of laughter flooded into the hall as if someone was being tickled.

Michael stood there amazed as the door on the clock swung open. Inside was a narrow passageway, just big enough for a boy his size to squeeze through. Michael could hear his mother finishing her phone conversation. There wasn't a moment to lose. With his heart pounding, he climbed into the clock and the door quickly closed behind him.

Slowly he crept along the slender corridor. When he reached the end he climbed down a ladder that led to a small tunnel. Michael crawled through on his hands and knees. Suddenly, WHEEE, the tunnel became a slide. Down he went,

round and round until, PLOP, he landed in the doorway of a magnificent dome-shaped room filled with hundreds of clocks. There were clocks of every size and shape and in the center of the room, hunched over a workbench, was an old man with wispy hair, painting numbers on the face of a delicate cuckoo clock.

"Hello, Michael!" the old man shouted, without looking up from his work. "We've been waiting for you. Please come in!"

Michael made his way through the crowded workshop and sat on the bench beside the peculiar man.

"Are you Grandpa?" he asked politely.

"Yes, yes, that's me. Grandfather T. T. for Time, that is. And this is my marvelous time factory." Then Grandfather T. turned away from his work, looked warmly into Michael's eyes and said, "My friends, the stars, told me about you, young man. I thought we had better have a chat. Can't have a boy like you going about without caring if he has a good time or not. You know, Michael," he whispered gently, "I'll tell you a special secret. Time is only what you make it. Life goes by in the wink of an eye and every precious minute counts."

With those words, cheers went up from all the clocks in the room, and Grandpa T. shouted, "So, let's not waste another second! Where's the cake?"

The cheering continued as a delicious looking chocolate cake, complete with brightly burning candles, appeared magically on the table. "Every birthday needs a Happiness Cake!" sang Grandpa T. as he and Michael danced about the room, shaking hands with all the clocks.

HAPPINESS CAKE

Chorus:
Ho Ho, Hee Hee, I'm Grandfather T.
And Happiness Cake is my specialty
So if you'd like to bake a Happiness Cake
Here's a marvelous recipe

A pinch of laughter and a dash of salt
Two cups of caring and some chocolate malt
A cupful of kindness, a teaspoon of glee
And some special fun powder, Yippee!
A tablespoon of friendship, some lemon drops
Stir it all up with some lollipops
Bake with a rainbow from above
But the best ingredient of all is . . . LOVE

Chorus

Happiness isn't something you can buy
You'll never find it sitting on a shelf
Happiness is something if you try
You can make the recipe yourself

Ho Ho, Hee Hee, all you need is time
And I'm sure your cake will turn out fine
Life is like a cake that only you can bake
And what you put inside is in the bite you take

A pinch of laughter and a dash of salt
Two cups of caring and some chocolate malt
A cupful of kindness, a teaspoon of glee
And some special fun powder, Yippee!
A tablespoon of friendship, some lemon drops
Stir it all up with some lollipops
Bake with a rainbow from above
But the best ingredient of all is . . . LOVE

Chorus

"I guess anyone can make a Happiness Cake," laughed Michael.

"That's the idea!" cheered Grandpa T.

Just then Michael heard his mother calling him.

"Shhh," whispered Grandpa T., and the noisy room was silent.

"You'd better be going, Michael. Here, take the shortcut." He opened a door in one of the grandfather clocks and there, to Michael's surprise, was an elevator. Reluctantly, Michael stepped inside and waved good-bye.

"Don't forget our secret," Grandpa T. smiled as Michael rode out of sight.

"Michael! Where have you been?" his mother exclaimed when she found him standing in front of the clock. "I've been looking everywhere."

In the living room Michael discovered a bunch of his old school friends from the city who had come to help him celebrate his birthday!

"SURPRISE!" they all hollered, as Michael's mom carried in an extra-large chocolate cake, complete with brightly burning candles!

That night Michael James Peabody fell into bed exhausted and content. With Grandpa T.'s secret tucked safely in his heart, he closed his eyes and whispered, "Thank you, stars."

TICK TOCK

Grandfather clock stands in the hall
It's very old and it's very tall
And though it is a stately sight
It never can tell the time just right

Chorus:
And it goes tick tock, tick tock
Tick, tick tock, tick tick tick
Tick tock, tick tock, tick tick tock

Sometimes it stops, sometimes it goes
And just what's wrong nobody knows
But every time that I pass by
It always seems to wink its eye

Chorus

Well, mother called the expert in
To see what he could do
He gave it a knock, and he gave it a shake
And the clock struck twenty-two

Chorus

Last night I heard the strangest thing
First a roar, then a ring
When I crept out of my bed
The clock was standing on its head

Chorus

This morning I discreetly tried
To open it and look inside
But a voice cried, "Ooooh, oh can't you see?
You're tick tock, tick tock, tickling me!"

Chorus

DO YOU KNOW WHAT MAGIC IS?

There were some kids and a short giraffe
Skipping along a crooked path
Close behind, a happy clown
Was gently tip-toeing around
Well, they came to a candy store
Bought some gumdrops and balloons
And turned into moons

   Chorus:

      Oh, do you know what magic is?
      Have you been to rainbow land?
      Or seen a dinosaur go sailing by?
      Any kid can help you try

There were some kids on a
      merry-go-round
They rode their ponies all over town
They had some birthday cake and pizza pie
Poor little Michael got an olive in his eye
Then they rode off in the wind
And called their wooden ponies
"Pepperonies"

   Chorus

There were some kids at a movie show
They took their seats and it started to snow
And then it rained all over the place
Poor little Jenny got ice cream on her face
Then they opened their umbrellas
And they flew off in the sun
Just having fun

   Chorus